Stuck That Way and Other Quandaries

Julie Kusma

ISBN: 978-1-7349039-3-5
juliekusma.com

CONTENT

STUCK THAT WAY

Published on CoffeeHouseWriters.com November 25, 2019

"Wow. How'd ya do that?" The boy appeared to have eyes like saucers.

"You've got to control your energy, son. Watch." His father's hand flashed back and forth from one material form to another. "When you perfect the technique, you can do... this."

"Whoa, your whole head changed! Super cool." He twisted and scrunched his face in contorted expressions, but held the same shape of himself.

The man laughed with delight at his young son's attempts to morph his appearance. His jubilation ceased the moment the boy's mother waltzed in and joined them.

"What are you two doing?" She smiled with fluidity.

"Nothing, dear. A little trick, that's all."

"Nothing? Jeepers, Dad, you did the best magic ever."

"Well, perhaps your father should perform for me. Don't you agree?" She eyed her husband with suspicion before she gazed down at her child. She ruffled the airy plume of hair on her son's head, puckered, and kissed his forehead.

"I don't believe your mother cares much for any of this."

"Oh, Mom. The trick is swell. Show her, Dad." He teetered on the edge of a clear, acrylic-like seat.

"Alright, something small, say, like this." The man let out a slow exhale. One by one, fingers popped out until an entire, flesh-colored hand manifested before them.

"ABSOLUTELY NOT." The mother jumped up, gripped her slender, ethereal hips and said, "I won't tolerate this behavior."

"But, Mom. It's…"

"Not allowed. End of discussion." She glared at her husband

"Oh, don't make a big deal out of nothing. We were having fun. Besides, what could happen?" He wiggled the encapsulated shape off.

The boy stared, eager for his mother's reply. He imagined what image she would display if she dared take one.

"You're well aware of what can happen." She turned away from him and straight toward her child. "Is that what you want— to frighten me?"

"No, Mom. But…"

"No buts. Some things one cannot undo." Her wisp of a finger wagged at him. "Do you understand me?"

"Of course, he does." The man smirked until he spotted his son somewhat hidden behind her. He shook his head in a plea not to practice now and waved for him to leave.

The boy squeezed with all his might. Small squares of matter materialized in the space one would consider a face.

"STOP THAT." She swished the air groping for him, but only

his essence remained.

"Relax, he's gone outside to play. Most likely, with the new kid next door."

"Promise me you won't teach him to do this. He pixelated! With a few more tries, a solid form might manifest. Honestly, I don't understand what you were thinking."

"Now, now, you're getting carried away. He retook his normal, light shape."

"Several boys have disappeared this week alone. I forbid this."

"Don't be silly. They haven't vanished." He moved toward the boundary of their dwelling and peered at the expanse designated as their lawn. "He's standing out front, and that new neighbor kid is headed over to him. He's fine."

Away from his mother's view, the boy struggled to replicate his father's trick.

"Hey," the new kid said as he approached. "What you doing?"

"Getting out of earshot of my parents."

"Were they arguing? I swear, your mom's shriek looms miles from your house."

"They call it a disagreement of opinions."

"Yeah, so, what were they fighting about?"

He stared at his new friend while he debated how much he should share. He glanced both ways. "Don't tell anyone, but my dad showed me how to make a corporeal form."

"No way."

"Yes way. Well, not an entire one, but he did a hand and a whole head."

"And he taught you how?"

"Kind of. He told me to control my energy. If I slow down enough, I will take a different shape."

He grimaced as he tried to create a face or even just a nose, but nothing happened. "Aw, I can't."

"You can," the neighbor kid said. "You made a couple opaque blocks of color wiggle in. Only for a second, but you did."

"Wait, for real?"

"Yeah, cross my heart."

"Have you ever done this before?"

"Naw," the new boy said. Behind his own back, fingers developed in a row like he was counting to ten. "I heard if you make an entire body, you go down there—automatic."

"W-w-why would I want to do that?"

"Are you kidding? Um, ice cream. Sunshine. Flowers. Everything."

"Ice cream?"

"Man, you don't know what ice cream is?" He studied the boy. "How about I pop down and nab some?"

"I thought you said you couldn't?"

He shrugged. "How hard can it be?" He spun into a luminous swirl of tornadic energy. He stopped with a bulbous face shoved out.

"Yikes! Hey, you scared me."

The kid pitched forward and grew lopsided like a stress ball head with its eyes popped out.

"Knock it off."

The head retracted into an acceptable size and tolerable construct. "I'm grabbing a triple-scooped cone of double-Dutch chocolate. If you're quick, when I'm back, you can steal a lick before it dissipates."

"Aren't you afraid of getting stuck holding that shape for so long?"

"Who told you that? Your mom?"

He nodded, yes.

"She just doesn't want you to enjoy yourself. I bet she hates when you have fun. Am I right?"

The boy reckoned he was correct. His eyes grew wide once again, like earlier when his dad did the trick. "Okay, do it."

The kid smiled with his novel, fashioned mouth, and evaporated without another word. He reappeared five seconds later. "Now," he yelled.

The boy flitted around in a desperate search of the vicinity. "Did I miss it?"

"Yeah. It was right here all cold and creamy and chocolatey." He shook off his form. "I guess you need a body for the full effect. Oh well, I gotta go. My mom said dinner was in ten, and I've been out here with you longer than that. See ya." The neighbor mocked the boy's gullibility as he donned a huge grin and strolled away.

Determined to harvest a bite for himself, he concentrated until his vibration slowed down, thick as mud. He opened his eyes and gazed at the dots of energy fluttering in and out around him. He had done it. He stood all flesh-and-bone

His spirit, now encased in this hardened, human form, stirred with the sense of being captive. Imprisoned. His appendages hung like lead tubes, and the gravity too strong to overcome.

He fought to lift each leg as he moved forward on the busy sidewalk in the noisy town. A cacophony of sensations overwhelmed and assaulted him. Harsh noises. Artificial light. Bright colors. Aching skin.

Panic quickened his breath. He was excited in an uncomfortable, anxious way, and he found it impossible to dissolve this solid shape.

"Mom?" His own croaky words scared him, and tears welled. "Dad?"

A flood of emptiness washed over the woman. "Something happened… to our son."

"Calm down."

"I can't. A mother just knows these things. He's gone."

The man ran to the window-like opening. "He's not there."

"What do you mean?" She paced with frantic movements. "I told you. I knew this would happen. He did your trick, and now he's trapped there."

"*If* he created a physical body, which is a monumental *if*, he can fix his energy. All he has to do is accelerate the frequency high enough that the earthly body can't exist. And poof, he's back here with us."

"Did you teach him that part?" She sneered, and her husband's aura dimmed. "I didn't think so."

"He can figure it out. He's a smart boy."

"Intelligence has nothing to do with it. The place is decadent. All those sensory inputs bombarding a flesh-covered nervous system. The Earth plane is outrageous. The mind assigns meaning to everything, and each person is sucked in."

"He's coming back. Everyone does— eventually."

The boy, in his alien form, stood alone in the unfamiliar world. He should have listened to his mother. She warned him he'd get stuck that way.

SOMETHING LURKING

Published on CoffeeHouseWriters.com in three parts on
September 2, 16, and 30, 2019

"Most Views" Winner September 2019

My house sits off a country road, miles from the nearest intersection, and even that road is remote. About three miles down on the left, my driveway juts off and wanders through the woods. Then the trees clear and give way to a full view of my house. Here, the days are quiet, barring the raps of woodpeckers and the cicadas' song. But, the nights take on a life of their own.

One hundred-fifty perennial species thrive on these densely wooded acres. Anything beyond the first few rows of trunks is impossible to observe when the leaves are full. The foliage veils the horizon. On moonless nights, the trees fade into the void of light. Eyesight becomes useless, and I must wait for my other senses to heighten, and sound to amplify. This is one of those nights.

My heart races, as I stand with my dog on my deck. We peer into the darkness. Every twig snap causes my imagination to scan through images of random woodland creatures, real or otherwise. Every crack of a branch triggers a survival response. Whatever lurks is right behind my house.

I rub my dog's head. "Boy? Did you hear something?"

He doesn't move. No muscles flinch. He freezes a few feet from my side, and we both stare at the blackness in silence.

"We're alright, boy." The words aim to reassure him, but his body doesn't yield.

Without warning, he flips an innate switch from cute pet to canine predator. A deep growl rumbles in his throat as he snarls. No one is safe out here—not tonight.

"Do your business, Finley," I whisper the command, wanting back inside my house.

The normal woodsy sounds I'm familiar with die off. No bugs buzz; no crickets chirp; no moths flutter around the glow of the bulb above the back door. *The light!* The illumination spotlights our position. I rush inside, flick off the light, and search for my dog through the screen.

The tiny squares of mesh are fragile and cannot offer any protection. My stomach knots. I don't want to go back out.

My cellphone buzzes and I slam the door shut before I register the hum is inside. The vibration scoots my phone across my dining room table and tumbles to the floor face up. A picture of my boyfriend smiles back at me.

"Hello... Of course, it's me... I don't know, tired, I guess... Finley needed to go out... Jordan, we heard something... You're right... I know, I'm acting silly... No, I don't want you to come over... Call me in the morning... Yeah, me too."

I toss my phone on the placemat and reopen the door, half expecting something to be on the other side. Nothing is, except a sheet of black, and I wait for my eyes to adjust. In the amount of time I take to enter my house and to talk to Jordan, my dog disappears from his last location. Without the light, the dark swallows him, but I don't turn the switch back on.

"Finley?"

My spit is hot, and I resist the urge to slam the door again, to lock the bolt, and to wedge a chair under the doorknob. None of these are choices I can make if I want to save him.

"Finley?"

The noises continue to emanate in the trees. They grow louder, more distinguishable, like underbrush crushing beneath footsteps. These movements come from something sizable. Something too big to be a distant neighbor's pet or a roving coyote. Several limbs break feet above the ground. The animal is tall, upright, like an enormous aberrant creature, or some deviant vagrant. I can't decide which one of those is worse. Both possibilities frighten me. Whatever is out there, stalks us.

The sharp snap of branches stops; the other sounds do not. The creature is past the rear clearing of my property, and now, in my yard. I'm unsure which, but it comes for my dog, or me. A painful whimper directs me toward Finley at the edge of the deck near the splits in the railing balusters.

If Finley lunges to attack, he will fall through the rail, off the decking, and down twelve feet to the ground below. All I want is his leash in my hand, so I can clip the metal clasp on his collar and persuade him back inside. But his leash hangs from a silver hook on the kitchen pantry door.

In the murkiness, I tiptoe toward Finley's last whine, and my heart pounds in my ears. Calm down. Predators feel the heartbeat as blood rushes through each vein. They smell their prey's fear, too. There! I spot my dog's shadowy form.

I cover my mouth, and his name quivers out, "Finley?"

My dog turns and gazes at me, no longer the wild, wolf-like killer, and no longer my beloved companion. Our eyes lock. He regards me, prayerfully, like his soul, is uncertain whether eternity exists. The glare of his eyes' blurs into a yellow smeary line.

"Finley!" I shriek, as I run toward him. My arms flail as I grasp for his legs… for his fur. He vanishes.

I'm not afraid anymore; I'm angry. Adrenaline pumps through my body and emboldens me to give chase. I listen as it drags my dog over to the left side of my lot. There's a place where the old barbed-wire fence lays in rust on the dirt; where the deer escape into the camouflage. Anything with any sense is as far away from here as possible.

I push my thumb down on the latch and pull the deck's gate open, and try not to create any unnecessary attention. I leave the gate ajar. I don't want a struggle when I return, because I'm not coming back without my dog.

Flagstone pavers provide access to the backyard. I move between the bunches of ornamental switchgrass and sneak down. The last stone wobbles. *Don't stumble.* Long blades of grass brush against my bare calves as my foot settles in the lawn. My toes find a mound of loose soil and sink in. Snakes live out here.

I never go outside at night. Never. Mosquitoes swarm to me like I'm a feast. If I do, I don't go out in my pajamas or without shoes. Not by choice. Yet, here I am, in a craze, tracking some animalistic biped back in the woods behind my house.

A stench hits me as I draw closer. *Metallic?* My mind searches to identify the odor. Blood. *Oh, God! Finley's blood.* The scent makes me more alert, and my night perception increases. An image emerges; a silhouette of the old abandoned building left by a previous owner and untouched by me. Vines engulf its exterior. The creature must plan to haul my dog to this outbuilding. The rickety old hut is a perfect shelter for a feral animal.

I must rescue Finley before this happens, and it devours him. If I step when the beast steps and breathe when it breathes, I can take Finley without detection. At least, I hope I can.

The massive animal-like thing will stop to swing the doors open—doors that dangle from rusty hinges. The rotten wood isn't strong enough to withstand a disturbance. Yet, the shed stands firm—all but the windows. Their panes knocked out in an incident long ago.

The moment the creature pauses, I will snatch Finley and race back to my house. He's heavy, but I will do it, like those people who lift cars off their loved ones or move boulders to free someone's leg. I will retrieve my dog and carry him to the safety of our home.

Finley's body drops with a lifeless thud, and I want him, but I wait for the monster to face the building. That's when I'll run. Only a few seconds remain before it turns around and tows its fresh kill inside.

My breath quickens. I'm ready. *Run now.* I dash to a nearby tree off to one side and pray I am unnoticed. Now. I sprint toward Finley, my arms out, ready to grab him and pull him away. *Just a few more feet. I can almost touch his legs.* I stretch further out and...

"Nooo!"

Leathery fists clamp my wrists, and I realize this is a trap. My arm pulls from the socket as it jerks me inside and throws me at the wall.

"Ugh!"

All air escapes my lungs as the left side of my back slams against the wooden windowsill. My rib cage breaks with a sickening crunch, and I collapse on the filthy cement. My mouth gapes open over a pile of decay, and a moldy bitterness mixes with my saliva. *Stand.* My body doesn't respond. *If I can force myself up, I... Might... Get... Out.*

I fight to get to my knees, and pain shoots through my spine. A vast paw-like hand obscures my vision before my cheek rips open. Claws dig deeper into my flesh and pierce my tongue.

The creature's other gigantic paw-hand punctures what's left of my chest cavity. My blood gurgles up, and I choke. This is it. We're not getting out.

One eye opens, and I glance over at Finley. His bloody body sprawls across the cold slab, inches from me.

My eyelid closes and a memory dances of me tossing a tennis ball, and him eager to catch the toy in his mouth. I spread my fingers out, reaching, stretching for him.

"Sorry boy." The words play in an endless loop, though my mouth doesn't move. My plea for forgiveness is an incoherent mumble. Not that it matters. Finley is dead; he can't hear me. But, I say it anyway.

My life clings to the gashes in my cheek. And I wait for the last drops of my blood to ooze out, heavy enough to break free and swim in the pool of red beneath me. Death brings relief.

I struggle to open my eyelids as they swell. All I can manage are two slivers of light. Even with puffy eyes, I find Finley's battered body. He is a few feet from me. I reach for him. My fingers stretch. They discover a hard clump in his hair and move past the dense, dry mat. I want the silkiness of his fur.

My eyes flutter and rollback. Each inhale drives a stab through my chest, and I pray for this to end. Traces of light shine through the empty window frame. I disregard my pain and embrace the sun's warmth on my skin. No last meal. No goodbyes. But, for a moment, I can have this. I take a deep breath. The summer air is full of the moss growing on the trees. This mixes with the earthiness of the bark upon which it cleaves. Both scents evoke wonder for life, and I am sad mine is ending. I take another long breath, and my eyes shoot open. *I'm alive!*

The cement floor no longer chills my bones. The agony racking my body reduces to silence. In fact, I don't feel anything—I sense my surroundings. Everything fills my awareness. Carpenter bees burrow tunnels in the planks on the backside of the shed. A distant neighbor's dog scratches at its owner's backdoor, and Mr. Beckley's alarm rings on his nightstand. *What the hell?* The old man's house is half a mile down the road.

I focus, cognizant of several— of five heartbeats from a wake of turkey vultures nearby. Feathers rustle as they launch. Each wing whooshes through the air, and they circle us overhead. Their unwavering patience is admirable. But, I don't much care for the anticipation they hold. These scavengers expect to thrust their beaks into my dog: their carrion.

Last night flashes, and I envision our attack. I force myself upright and cringe as I recall the puncture to my lungs. I hunt for injuries. *How can I breathe?*

Another image flickers, and I wince. *My face.* My tongue surveys the inside of my cheek. Nothing. My fingers travel the outer surface, like a blind person, I canvas my face. *Impossible.* There are no open wounds. No slashes.

Something did happen to us; I didn't dream it. Because, I'm not in bed under my bear paw quilt, and my dog isn't asleep at my feet. We're outside, in the old rickety outbuilding. I crawl over to Finley. *Here's my proof.* He is dead. My hand hovers above his head. Arterial splatter colors the cement a dull shade of crimson. No dream—this is a nightmare; I should be dead too.

My lips sink into his muzzle, and I kiss him. I press my mouth to his nose. Cold. Dry. *How can I live without you?* I sit back on my heels. *They won't eat you, I promise.* I need to bury him. But not near the woods; I won't make him spend eternity there. Instead, I choose the side of the house by the gum tree. The one with the Indian-like carvings which scar the smooth, pale bark. Finley loves this spot.

My pajamas soak my tears as I cradle my face in the fabric and prepare for the deed.

"Get the shovel. Dig a hole." My voice is rotund—more profound and sends goosebumps over my flesh. It belongs to someone else. *It's okay.* I want someone to tell me what I need to do.

I move, programmed, not thinking, just doing, and stare at Finley. His lifeless form heaps at my feet. I step to his other side. Somehow, he's more substantial than I remember. He weighs a hundred pounds, but all soft. *Too many treats.* I laugh and wipe the snot bubble from my nose. *You only live once, right boy?*

Body fluids encrust his hair, and his curls are smooth waves across his muscles. He is massive and muscular: ripped. Each ridge glistens under the morning sun. A tremendous urge to snatch him up overwhelms me, but something causes me to stop. Finley isn't the same. He's different from the alive Finley. My desire to embrace him disappears as an equal amount of fear wells in my gut. He's no longer my dog.

The chest heaves.

In those coroner shows, they say gases often trap inside the lungs and the stomach. Sometimes the corpses move for up to half a day. The digestion continues. The nails still grow, and the bladder and bowels release.

A squeak escapes some orifice in his body. And, he appears to—reanimate. I cradle both temples and shake my head. *Not possible.*

Finley's eyes snap open. *He's alive?* I drop, and my knees smack the concrete with all my weight, but there is no pain.

"Finley?"

He growls because he doesn't know who I am. His throaty snarl intensifies, and he's on his feet, ready to strike. The force of his assault knocks me on my back. His large front paws pin me to the ground as his chartreuse eyes pierce mine. Their hue is unnatural. I turn away, and without intention, expose my jugular vein. He bares his teeth and drool hits my throbbing neck.

"Finley, it's me." My voice remains fuller than usual. He still can't identify me.

A cavernous rumble finds a way through his clenched teeth. He is ferocious: savage, like the thing in the woods. He lunges, but I grab fistfuls of fur on his throat and block his assault. I struggle to fend him off, because he's strong, and he's doing his damnedest to get at me.

"Down, boy!"

The pressure of his weight on my arms stops. I relax my hands, but keep my fingers ready. Finley leans down and runs his tongue across my face the same way he did as a puppy. He snarls and licks again. He vacillates between beast and dog. Finley isn't a puppy, or even a canine anymore. My pet is more like an enormous gray wolf, except his hair isn't gray, and he's way too massive for a wolf. He's more like some supersized prehistoric beast. One with vicious eyes which glow behind blood-matted bangs.

I hesitate, uncertain if I can pet him. He lets me, and I take the opportunity to examine his body. Finley doesn't have any wounds either. I glance at his blood all over the shed's floor. Somehow, we've both healed ourselves, quicker and beyond what is possible. *What's happening to us, boy?*

Finley replies without a bark. We communicate through telepathy, and he agrees. We are no longer the same as before; we are something quite different.

Come. I say the command in my head. We need to take refuge inside. He comprehends and leaps next to the doors and waits for me to open them.

The morning light blasts my skin with a newfound intensity. The thought of being a vampire crosses my mind. But, I don't burst into flames, or crumble in a pile of ashen dust. Finley tells me he might be a dire wolf or a werewolf. Most likely, a combination of the two. *I'm not a weregirl, am I?* I'm not, then again, I'm not human anymore either.

The vultures leave. They only consume fresh, dead meat, and although we both were dead, now we are undead. I step into the clearing of my backyard. My movements alert all living things of our dangerous proximity. The wildlife scatters, flies away, or burrows deeper underground. The typical outdoor noises disappear like last night when the creature approached us. *What are we?*

My head jolts to my left side as I register the chitter of a squirrel. *Oh, poor creature. You should run.* Finley growls behind me, and I understand he plans to catch this dumb animal and eat it whole. I slam the shed doors, trapping my dog, my wolf-like companion inside. Stay.

Finley rams the door. The latch can't hold him. He wants to dart through the woods and massacre everything he encounters. *He's hungry.*

I pull a metal sign off the building's siding, bend it in half, and slip it through the doors' handles. The makeshift lock won't last for long. I must move fast.

Instincts take over, and I'm down, close to the ground in a runner's start. The grass is so vibrant, so green and the dirt is a sandy mix. I can smell the river in it. The intensity is distracting. So, I shut my eyes and sense the life energy around me. I don't need to see.

In seconds, I'm off and clench a squirrel in my teeth. The entrails pour into my mouth, and an urge to rip the rodent apart surges. I fight my craving and don't allow myself to eat the thing. My jaw opens, and the tattered carcass falls in my hands. A savage kill. The monster from last night flashes in my mind.

Four more squirrels die in my brutal hands. Before I realize what I'm doing, my claw-like nails pierce through their throats. So, I poke one dead thing's body through the slit in another's neck. A sling of death, I wear over my shoulder.

Finley detects this odor as I approach, and he stops his

assault on the doors.

I crack the door and fling the meal down. Unrestrained, he consumes all five rodents in less than a minute. His ferocity disgusts me because I slay them in this same manner. Residue sticks to my tongue, and I spit the pieces of hair bound in blood and bowel on the ground. I pull the doors open. *Come.* I wipe the back of my hand across my mouth.

Satisfied, Finley obeys. He follows me to the house. I point, and we both jump the twelve feet up to the deck without a running start.

The broken balusters in the railing remind me how brutal, how cruel the beast had slaughtered us. *That's what we are.* A tuft of black fur, dark like coal, glistens from where the splintered wood traps it, and I pull it free.

Finley sniffs the clump of hair in my hand, and I'm sure he's set to track down our attacker. I acquire the scent, and I agree. I want to find the creature, the one that turned us into these unhuman things. Our eyes dart toward the tree line.

"Heard you yelling for your dog last night. Everything alright?"

The monstrous part of me rumbles. Human thoughts intertwine with animal instinct. I remember speaking with my boyfriend last night. I pray he hasn't come to check on me. The intimacy of our relationship makes me fear my ability to stay in control.

I spot a man at the edge of the tree line. He points at us, and his yellowed nails and knotty knuckles gain most of my attention. The rest of my brain sizes him up.

The intruder isn't Jordan.

The middle-aged man steps out of the trees and stands inside my yard. He's over sixty and overweight. He's all geared up in Mossy Oak camo hunting attire fresh off the rack, and he reeks of synthetic doe urine sprayed from a can. The unnatural stench hangs in the air around him and ruins his chance of bagging any deer, or anything else.

I grab Finley's scruff. He's jittery, dying to sprint across the lawn and devour the man like he's a big fat woodchuck. I raise my other hand, a signal for the man to stop where he's at.

"Don't..." My voice is guttural, and I don't know how to flip the wild part of me off. I try again, "Don't come any closer."

"You okay, lady?"

Finley yanks against my hand, so I tighten my grip. "Yeah, I'm good," I holler back, "just a little under the weather."

"Your dog under the weather, too?"

With this man in his sight, my wolf dog's energy quickens. The vibration travels from his scruff to my hand. He's ready to act but waits.

Sun-burnt leaves unfold as the weight of a heel lifts. Stiff fabric swishes and confirms the movement. The old fool steps into the clearing.

Finley breaks free and bounds off the deck. I give chase. Halfway to his kill, I realize, I can't catch him. The old man fumbles an attempt to arm himself. My dog lunges.

He knocks the man flat on the ground, and I fall on all fours next to them. Finley sinks his long cuspids into the hunter and tears the flesh open. The man's arms thrash in desperation. A piece of vocal cord rips through the slit in his throat. He chokes on the spurts of fluid that escape.

Blood carries a distinctive odor. A carnivore is more intense than the herbivore. This hunter, with skin like tanned hide, is a meat-eater. Yet, he offers the slightest sweetness, and this intoxicates me. Unable to resist, and without any thinking, I join the feast. I exchange growls with Finley like we're two pack mates who must remind each other to share.

I sit back for a moment. My hunger for this human's blood makes me reconsider whether I am a vampire, after all. Except, I have more to quench than thirst. I eat the body, too.

My new skills are a close match for Finley's. I suppose vampires are quick and possess keen sensory abilities. But, if Finley is right, and he turns into the canine's common ancestor, the dire wolf, I can't be like him. Not completely. *What's the oldest version of homo sapiens?*

I glance at the wolf-like animal beside me. Red drips from our mouths and paints our chins. Ancient genetics. The creature from the woods, its DNA infects us and triggers the expression of something primordial within us. Recessive. Dormant. Lurking.

The creature's ape-like hands come to mind. Melanistic: covered in black hair with black skin. Hominin. I hold my hands out. Each of my fingernails rises, thick like claws, and taper to fine points. I recall the monster's talon-like nails.

A species from an undiscovered branch, existing before the lineage splits into Neanderthals and Denisovans. Some unidentified hominid taking a path of its own. An ancestral crossbreed comprised of different animals. Something unnatural like the immortal jellyfish which rebirths over and over, forever.

My lust for blood and my cannibalistic desire makes me wonder if this unknown line is the origin of all mythical beings. The missing link. A supernatural chimera, undead and in the flesh.

Finley sits back to lick his paw. I grab the hunter by one leg, above what used to be his ankle, and drag him in the trees. For a second, remorse sweeps in. I didn't sense him anywhere around here last night. I recall my teeth as they tore his muscles from his bones. No shame, he was dead when I took my first bite. The vultures circle overhead. *Go ahead, eat what's left.*

I point at the deck. Finley joins me as I head inside. This time, when I jump, light-headedness blurs my vision. I'm still turning. I open the back door and lean against the casing. Finley trots toward the living room and curls up on the sofa for a nap.

The half bath is down the hall. I stagger in and support myself on the sink and turn the faucet on. The water runs like liquid ice, but I splash my face and glance up. I didn't expect the mirror to reflect lucent, sallow skin. Blue lines squiggle under the surface. Hunter's blood dry on my lips. I move closer. The whites of my eyes now pink, each iris citron like Mt. Dew and my pupils retract into tiny dots. Anyone of these features horrific, but when they combine in one face, they create a grotesque display.

I scrub the blood from my mouth. The translucent red water

swirls in the porcelain basin and streams down the drain. My stomach churns. I'm not sure I can survive the full transformation.

My wolf dog snarls from where he lies in the front room. He springs up, and the sofa tips with the force of his hind legs, and crashes back. He clicks on the wood floor as he races through the house on a predator's prowl.

"Finley!" *What the hell's going on?*

I turn too quickly, and the dizziness returns. I flip the toilet seat up, and puke chunks of flesh, muscle, and fat. My body purges the foreign contents. I'm not ready for that type of meal. Tears run from both eyes, and I wish the mortal part of me would hurry up and die.

The backdoor latch clicks and the door squeaks open. My heart pounds in my chest as I register the heartbeat of the human who enters my home. His scent is familiar. *Oh, gawd! Jordan!*

I push myself up, knowing I must stop Finley. My eyes open. Remnants float on the water's surface, and I heave again.

Finley growls down the hallway. He passes the bathroom and moves around the corner where he can stalk the intruder—my boyfriend—his next kill.

Thick, leathery skin and digestive acids rush up my throat in unrelenting repetitive regurgitation. Bright pinkish-red tissue swims around the vomit, and I realize my stomach lining is coming up too.

"Jackie? You home?"

"Go, Jordan. Please." I struggle to push the words out. "We're sick."

"What the hell happened?"

He's not listening to me—he never does. His voice moves closer.

"Did Finley attack you?"

"Stay back. You need to leave." My voice quivers. Whatever emotions linger in me, now traipse over the undertones of the predator within.

"Babe, blood is everywhere— out back—all over the door. I'm calling an ambulance.

"NO!" I grunt the word like an animal just learning to speak.

I pinpoint Finley's location as he rumbles a low-pitched growl. He moves around the corner and pauses at the other end of the hall, opposite Jordan.

"For chrissake!" Jordan stumbles backward. He bumps into the Hoosier cabinet behind him and the china clinks together. One of the cabinet's glass doors pops open. The blue, porcelain rabbit tumbles and breaks on the floor. "What's wrong with your dog? Does he have rabies?"

Finley glares down the hallway at Jordan, and I sense no familiarity with my boyfriend remains. To Finley, he's meat.

I reach for the bathroom doorknob. Finley understands what I'm about to do. He continues to growl, but he steps back. When I open the door, I'm between the two of them. The door shields me from Jordan's view.

"Jackie?"

I glance over my shoulder, and Finley locks eyes with me. He whimpers, tucks his tail, and cowers back. My appearance frightens him.

I push the door too hard, and the cheap, brass knob hits the wall. Jordan's got the hunter's Remington. He aims the rifle at me.

"What the…?"

Jordan's name grumbles from my lips in an incoherent garble.

He pulls the bolt back. "What the hell kind of sickness does that?" The lever swooshes forward, and down.

I hiss as I bare my long, sharp fangs. My hands are ape-like with talons for nails. The same inky, coarse hair of the creature grows in random patches along my arms. Soon, this fur will cover me. I glance at myself in the mirror. The monster from the woods glares back at me. I am an apex predator—the supernatural chimera.

A bullet zings past my left side. I tell Finley to hide. He obeys, running on the other side of the house and out the backdoor. Before I can turn back around, another shot cracks from the barrel. The projectile shatters on impact at the base of my skull. Fragments of bone penetrate my brain and severe my spinal cord. *Sorry, boy.* This time, there's no coming back for me.

BY INDUCTION

Published on CoffeeHouseWriters.com October 24, 2019

The heavyset woman stormed inside with such force, the front door swung into the wall, ricocheted, and slammed shut behind her. "Judd, you're not gonna believe this."

She raced through their house, dodged the TV tray in the center of the living room, and entered their kitchen. "Judd?"

Her frantic quest ended when she reached their turquoise Frigidaire. "I swear you don't listen to a damn thing, least not when I want you to."

She plucked her tattered apron from the hook. The straps disappeared as she cinched the material around her waist. Opposite the fabric draped on her front, a lopsided bow emerged on her back.

Her plump fingers grabbed the chrome-plated handle. Vapor billowed from the appliance, a reaction to the room's warmer temperature. She pushed both her polyester sleeves up and removed the items.

Boxes of frozen entrees found themselves tossed on the counter. The pints of ice cream came next. First, the pistachio, her husband's favorite, followed by hers, strawberry.

By the time Judd entered the room, she had plowed past the

containers of Thanksgiving leftovers. She had pulled out the plastic baggies of chicken chili con carne, three-meat cannelloni, and the beige stuff she believed to be tuna bake.

Judd paused halfway to the kitchen sink. "What on earth?"

"My jars." She glanced over at her husband's pale face.

Her eyes darted to his slippers. A toe wore the lining thin and threatened to poke through the outer corduroy fabric. While she had been at work, he had never changed from his bedclothes. "Are you alright?"

"I'm fine." He flicked his wrist like a bothersome fly invaded his space. "Got a little heartburn, that's all."

The blue top on the antacids popped open with a push of his thumb. Three chalky tablets tumbled to his hand. With the cold water turned on, he filled a cup. "Jars of what?"

"Names." She tugged on the fixed package of rib roast. "Hand me a knife."

He took a utensil from the silverware drawer and handed the butter knife to his wife. "We've got names — in jars — in our freezer?"

"I told you." Her eyes narrowed, and her lips tightened. "Patricia? She gets rid of people she doesn't like."

Judd's wiry eyebrows raised. "Ain't she the lady from work you hate?"

His wife nodded as she pried between the ice formed underside and the hard hunk of meat. "She put one of her neighbor's names in the freezer and next thing, the house sold, and the pesky woman moved out."

"Ridiculous. She didn't make the person leave town any more than she's in here making my dinner." Judd laughed, which turned into a choke, followed by a violent bout of coughing.

His wife walked over to him and placed the back of her hand across his forehead. "What's your explanation?"

"A coincidence." He swatted his wife's hand. "She got a promotion or won the lottery. Anything but what you imagine happened."

"You catching something?"

Judd shook his head. "Come on." He gave her a gentle nudge. "Clean this mess up and fix us dinner."

"In a minute." His wife waddled back to her task and added defrosting to her mental list of things that needed to be done.

Chunks of white frost broke free as she jabbed at the mounds of built-up frost. "Some of the girls didn't believe her either. So, she asked us to select somebody for her to eradicate." She continued to chip.

"I'm taking the bait. Who'd ya pick?"

"Ernestine from accounting." She wiggled the knife back and forth that she wedged under the roast. The pinkish, ice-covered meat released, and she lifted the package.

"That a roast?" Judd rubbed the side of his face and circled his lower jaw.

The frozen block hit the countertop with a loud thunk. "A week after Patricia condemned the woman's fate by pen, she was gone. No one ever saw her again."

"Patricia or Ernestine?" He sat at their speckle-topped table and sipped his water.

"Ernestine!" She waved the knife at him. "Always got to sit in the broken chair? The other three are like new."

"This one ain't broke yet. Just a little worn like me." He gave his wife a crooked smile. "Guess I can zap one of those pre-made deals in the microwave."

"If your backside hits the linoleum, don't ask me to help you up."

"Never would. You're too busy killing everyone off."

She gingerly scrapped under one of the jars anchored in the ice.

"So, you decided to doom a few people for yourself." He bent his left elbow and rotated the same side's shoulder. "My arm aches. Might be the flu."

The center jar popped loose. She unscrewed the metal lid. Two wrinkled fingers, like tweezers, clasped the piece of torn paper and raised the vexation out. "Oh, Judd." She held the scrap for her husband to read. Black ballpoint letters spelled out the name of her best friend.

"Why, Betty?"

"She told everybody my sugar cookie recipe came from a magazine."

Judd rolled his eyes.

"Well, she lied. So, I wrote her name down. I shoved her in the freezer right behind the prime rib I've been saving for a special occasion. I cursed her, and now... she's dead."

"Betty passed away?" He fiddled with the band of aluminum along the table's outer edge.

"The girls at work told me she died from an aneurism last night. I killed her."

Judd rubbed his mouth. "Ain't that something? I ran into her at the grocery the other day. Damned if I knew I'd never see her alive again." He placed both hands on the table and pushed himself up. "Well, I guess you got your occasion. You can make something fancy with the roast for her wake."

"I don't care if you don't believe me."

"Where's the aspirin?"

"In the same place, they've been in for the past twenty years."

Judd's expression turned sour.

"They're in our medicine cabinet."

She studied her husband as he braced himself with the chair's back. "I did do it, and here's proof.

An old woman lived on our block when I was a kid. Everyone thought she was crazy, but I understood her wickedness. I caught her spying on me while I played outside. I hadn't done anything wrong. So, I glared right back at her and screamed, I hope you die."

"So, you're saying you wished the old woman down the block dead, and the old lady died like old people do?"

"Judd Clark, sometimes I hate you. I wish… I wish you would hurry up and…"

He stammered back, grabbed his chest, and moaned as he fell

against the kitchen's yellow wall.

"Oh, I take them back." She rushed to his side. "I didn't mean those words."

He staggered a few feet, slumped over the cabinet, and laughed. His face turned beet red, and sweat glistened on his upper lip.

"Damn you, Judd. Not funny." She smacked his arm and walked away. "Now, I do want you dead."

"You can't wish death upon somebody and make them drop. Be a violation of free will and all, don't you think?"

"Well, perhaps the laws of nature only apply to the rest of you. All I know is, I cursed a few people, and two died."

"Maybe you can use your supernatural powers for good instead of evil and fix dinner."

His wife huffed, returned to the Frigidaire, and pulled out another jar.

"You ought to throw the damn things away." He flinched and brought his hand to his chest. "Be in the front room when you get done with this nonsense."

She unscrewed the metal ring and read another name. This curse was for the dry cleaner. She considered throwing it out, but spun the lid tight, and placed the jar back in the freezer. They had ruined her favorite blouse.

Their kitchen was in disarray. She shoved the roast back inside, stacked the somewhat thawed entrees on the left, and tossed the mushy, bagged leftovers to the right. The containers of stuffing and roasted turkey, she threw in the trash. "I'm making supper, now," she hollered into the living room.

The recliner made a thud. Judd had moved the lever back in the fully reclined position.

She opened the loaf of white bread. Ham and swiss cheese sandwiches would have to suffice. After all, she was mourning the loss of her best friend.

She tore the chip package and dropped a generous handful on Judd's plate. "Pickle?" He didn't reply. She gave him a dill spear anyway, not because he liked them, but because it made the meal more appetizing.

"Here you go." She sat his dinner on the stand. "Your supper's ready."

Her husband didn't budge. She lugged the tray across the carpet. Chips fell from the plate along the bumpy ride, and when she was close enough, she smacked his leg. "Wake up."

Judd remained still. She leaned over, and half expected him to open his eyes and scare the tar out of her. He didn't move. Not then, not ever again.

Twenty minutes later, an ambulance arrived.

One paramedic waited near the front door, and in between radio communications, he declared Judd dead. The other attendant asked if her husband had shown any signs of cardiac arrest.

Her eyes were blank as she stared at the man.

"Did he have chest pains, discomfort in his arms, or in his jaw? What about indigestion?"

She gazed past him, only seeing their freezer. "No. I don't think so." She tried to recall if she had ever condemned Judd by pen.

"Ma'am, nothing would have saved him."

She didn't say anything, because she understood that wasn't the truth. She should have checked all the jars, or thrown them away like he told her to do.

After the men carried her late husband out of her home, she marched to the kitchen. She pulled everything back out in haste. The food hydroplaned on the condensation formed from its earlier near thaw, and slid across the floor.

She stabbed at the ice until a previously unopened jar was liberated. This container stored her beautician's name. The next one, the butcher's. Only one remained unchecked.

The knife hit the glass. Cracks spidered upon impact. Her hands trembled as she prayed she was wrong about the name doomed inside.

Both hands unfolded the scrap, and her greatest fear realized as she revealed her husband's name. She released the paper and gazed as it floated down like a feather, weightless, and free.

The top sheet of the grocery notepad tore loose without much effort, and she cursed herself as the pen she held scribbled her own name. DEIDRE.

The butcher's name shook out, and she planted her accordion scrap inside.

She spun the lid down and placed the jar back on ice. Three of the letters remained visible through the glass. Judd would appreciate the humor, she thought as she read D-I-E.

The door closed and sealed her fate. She sat in her husband's favorite chair and waited for her own demise.

THAT'S CREEPY, SANTA!

Published on CoffeeHouseWriters.com December 9 and 25, 2019

"Most Views" Winner December 2019

Christmas often brings joy, and other times, sadness. For Maya, the holiday meant the entertainment of her mother-in-law. Plus, the forced endurance of a long list of complaints. Where this woman was concerned, she would never be perfect for her son.

But, this was the night before that whole disaster would unfold. Tonight, she and Paul would exchange gifts with each other. Alone. The two of them. Fireplace. Wine. Maybe more. Maya smiled to herself, taking in the aroma of burnt wood which filled the night.

She wiped her shoes on the *Ho! Ho! Ho!* doormat, slipped the house key into the lock, and stepped inside, quiet like a mouse.

The warm, indoor air caused tiny clumps of snow to melt and slide across her skin. Her entire body shivered as the chill of winter shook free.

Maya took her heels off and tossed them aside. Next, she hung her pink, faux fur coat on the hook in their mudroom. Balanced on one leg, she used her stocking-covered arch to dry the other foot. Maya peered around the corner. She didn't see her husband.

"Paul?" She tiptoed across the kitchen floor. A huge grin formed. She imagined the expression on his face after he unwrapped the negligée she had purchased exclusively for him.

"In here," he called from their living room.

Logs crackled and popped in the fireplace. An amber glow set the perfect mood for their private Christmas Eve. She anticipated their encounter all week, and now she was prepared for a night neither of them would forget.

Toward the next room, she snuck. Maya wanted to see him for just a moment, undetected. She smoothed her short, wool skirt as she advanced, and readied herself for a dramatic entrance.

No sooner had she reached the dining room, she spotted a package on the center of their table. She knew exactly who this was from, and her glee transformed into bitterness. She marched past the gift.

"Did your mother bring that here today?" Maya glanced back and pointed at the box before she turned with a glare back at him.

"Yeah, I guess so." Paul stood and sauntered toward her. "I found it at the front door when I got home." He looked at her like a cat about to catch a canary. "Tonight's the night. Ready for your present?"

"Not until you throw that thing out."

"I can't put mom's gift in the trash."

Maya scowled at her husband. His momma-boyishness sickened her.

"Come on, baby." He waltzed over and seized her hips with both hands and attempted to pull her close.

She resisted, turned her head, and curled the corner of her mouth in disgust.

"What if she got us something nice this year?"

"Your mother never buys us anything we like."

"I kind of like the trout mounted on the fake wood plank. Sang a half a dozen songs, I think."

"You mean the one I torched outside in the firepit?"

"Nooo. Is that what happened to it?"

Her eyes drew into small penetrating dots.

"Alright," he said, as he raised his hands in surrender. "You can burn, sell, or throw it off a cliff. I don't care, but not until after she leaves tomorrow. Deal?"

This was a small victory. Maya would only have to tolerate the item, and the woman, for a few hours the next day. She nodded.

Paul winked at her and offered a charming grin. "We should unwrap the damn thing. Let's put this drama behind us, and move on with our night."

A soft smirk instantly responded. "Yeah, okay."

"Fantastic. Want some wine?"

"In a minute." She flicked a torn edge with her index finger. "The paper isn't even new. There are wrinkles everywhere." She leaned down for a closer inspection. "She used the candy cane paper I wrapped her present in a couple of years ago."

"Naw."

"Yeah, we bought her a blender. I swear if she gifted it back to us, I'm going to kill her." She was joking, but the way she said the words insinuated malice.

She slid the package over in front of herself and loosened the ribbon with one pull. The piece of holly-green satin fell to the table. The lid had been wrapped separately. So, she lifted the top off the box and revealed a reddish fabric nested inside.

"What is it?" Paul asked.

"I don't know. A pillow." She reached down to retrieve the stuffed item and grabbed with both hands. "OUCH." She flinched and dropped the ugly thing before she shoved her finger into her mouth. A drop of blood had been drawn.

"What happened? Did it bite you?" He leaned in to look for himself and chuckled.

"Very funny. It's not alive." She gingerly took hold and lifted. Two, red, beady eyes stared back at her. She released the doll once again. "Gross, she gave us a scary-looking Santa." A shudder ran through her as she pushed the box toward Paul.

He grabbed the corner and dragged the package across the table, closer to himself. He laughed out loud as he took the tip of the faded red hat. "A stuffed Santa?" He examined the surface. "You must have been stabbed by a pin." He turned the doll and winced at its face. White, curled hair formed the trim on the cap and jacket. Two thick, painted on eyebrows framed the ceramic bulbs inserted below. "The eyes are a little weird."

"Weird? Downright disturbing is more appropriate." She recoiled as her husband spun it around and pretended to make it talk.

"Merry Christmas, little girl," he said in a higher-pitched voice.

"Stop it. That's creepy."

"Don't you mean, that's creepy, Santa?"

"Get it out of here. NOW."

"Maya," Paul said with his natural tone, "we can't dispose of this."

"I know, she's coming tomorrow, but after that. You promised me, Paul."

"No, I meant ever. This is a holiday decoration. Mom will expect us to decorate with it every Christmas."

"Every...year... until she dies?"

"I'm afraid so." He gave her a crooked smile. "I just don't understand why she bought this."

"And, why wouldn't she wait until tomorrow?" Maya clenched her teeth. "How old is the old bat, again?"

Paul shook the fluffed creature as he contemplated the strange gift. "Don't let this stupid doll spoil our evening."

"Oh, the night is already ruined." She moved around the table to avoid both and headed for their kitchen.

"Are you leaving? I have something special for you in the other room."

"I'm pouring myself a stiff drink. If you think there's a chance of you getting lucky tonight, you're wrong. I don't care how amazing your gift for me is..." She jabbed her finger at the washed-out lump clutched in his hand. "While that thing is in our house, you're getting the cold shoulder."

"Well, damn." He studied the plastic face. "Hey, pour me a drink too."

He stared in the doll's red, bulb-like eyeballs. "Apparently, the only warmth for me tonight is from booze. Thanks a lot," he mumbled. The Santa's grin appeared more menacing, and he thought the eyes glowed. He gazed into the depth of the bulb-eyes and pulled the face closer to his. A brilliant flash stunned him, followed by a wisp of smoke. The smoky substance twisted upon itself and darted into Paul.

Alone in the kitchen, Maya took a glass from the cabinet. With a sigh, she grabbed a second one, which she sat down a little hard. From the freezer, Maya scooped a handful of ice and divided the cubes among the two highball glasses. Bourbon sounded about right. So, she snatched the neck of the Maker's Mark on the counter and removed the cap. Maya poured two fingers of the golden liquor into his.

An idea made her pause. Paul's treasured cognac was hidden on the top shelf of their pantry. A gift from his father the last year he had spent the holidays with them. She dumped her ice into the sink and set the glass down. She planned to open his prized bottle out of spite.

At their pantry, she lifted herself up on her toes to reach to the back of the shelf. Her shirt raised as she stretched, and a soft groan escaped her lips as her fingertips grazed the bottle. She strained further, slightly higher, and maneuvered the round, stout container to pivot toward her. With each swipe from her middle finger, the cognac moved closer until the etched label came into full view. Frapin XO VIP Cognac, she whispered to herself. She only hoped the stuff was as good.

An uneasiness surged, and she pondered whether she should do this.

A gurgling, raspy moan emanated from behind her.

Maya rolled her eyes. "Paul…" She snagged the bottle and lowered herself on her heels. "Don't even try it, mister." She turned to face him. "If you think…" The bottle fell from her hand. Glass shattered on the floor.

Paul glared at her. His eyes glowed with a reddish hue, and his smile grew into an evil one. His face had taken on the same expression as the one on the creepy Santa doll.

She grabbed the reindeer-headed bottle-opener from the counter and held the antlers out, like a weapon. "Paul, what's wrong with you?"

"Time for your present."

***

Juice oozed from the roast and sizzled against the hot pan as Maya removed Christmas dinner from their oven. The meaty aroma, combined with the seared, liquified fat, filled the air with an odd, unidentifiable odor.

Maya jabbed the carving fork deep and raised the cooked chunk over to a platter. She wiggled the utensil free, only to stab the prongs in the top of the meat and held it in place. The electric knife buzzed as she carved serving-size slabs, careful not to mar the plate's gold-painted edge. As she sliced, clouded broth puddled over the embossed hollies, and threatened to spill on the counter.

Warmed rolls, steamed broccoli, and honey-glazed carrots rounded out their holiday meal. Paul always requested some manner of Russet potatoes. None were prepared. She was confident he wouldn't mind the absence of his beloved nightshades this year. She placed the platter at the center of the table where yesterday, an unexpected package waited.

Two bottles of wine flanked the left side of the buffet. One white and one red, both were ready for uncorking. As Maya inspected her festive array, she realized she had forgotten something. The reindeer-headed bottle opener was absent. She hurried back to the kitchen and retrieved the item from the dish rack. Now, everything appeared perfect. Maya closed her eyes and relished her contentment with all she had accomplished.

The doorbell rang. Not once. Not twice. But repeatedly, until Maya swung the front door open.

"What took you so long? I would have frozen to death had it been any longer." Paul's mother stepped inside, turned around, and cleared her throat. This signal, which Maya found annoying, indicated the woman disapproved of something, or required attention. In this instance, she awaited the removal of her winter jacket.

Maya reached for the sleeve and smiled as the woman flinched at her touch. "Merry Christmas, Margaret." She laid the coat over the back of a nearby chair.

"What is that gawdawful stench?" Margaret's hand pressed against her nose in an attempt to block further intrusion.

"Would it matter? I could tell you it was a prime rib or a human rib cage, your reaction would be the same."

Maya strolled to the dining room table, pulled out the head chair, and sat down.

"Where's Paul? Why didn't he greet me like he always does?"

"He didn't feel like himself last night, and today, he can't quite pull himself together."

Maya opened her napkin and draped the stiff, white cloth across her lap. "Be a dear and open the front bottle." She pointed at the Cabernet, not sure of the appropriate pairing, but somehow this choice struck her as dead-on.

Margaret, taken by surprise with her daughter-in-law's boldness, went to the buffet as ordered. She grabbed the opener. A dark, reddish-brown substance stained the crevices and further defined the fur on the brass animal head. She fiddled with her grasp, unsure of how to hold the tool without jabbing the antlers into her palm. She sighed and turned toward Maya. "Where's my son? If you're unwilling to serve the wine, he should do it. Where are your manners? I'm a guest in your home."

"He's here, but he won't be taking a seat at the table." Maya stood and waltzed over to pour herself a glass of the red liquid she desired. "Sit down, and we'll eat before it gets cold."

Margaret stepped aside. "I'm not eating without him." She headed across the living room toward the hallway.

"I wouldn't do that. He's a mess." She took a sip.

Maya grinned as Margaret glanced back. She counted on the old woman not listening.

Margaret continued her search. Her steps quickened as she neared the open master room door. "Paul, are you alright?" If she expected to find her son curled under a comforter and sick, she was wrong. The bed was empty and perfectly made.

Light streamed from under the closed bathroom door, and the exhaust fan hummed with a rattle. Margaret entered the bedroom. "Paulie? It's your mother." No response.

This time, she knocked on the door. Nothing.

Margaret's hand quivered as she reached for the knob. She turned and pushed the door open.

The mirror reflected a splatter of something pinkish-red on the tile wall. Margaret rushed in, grabbed the shower curtain, and yanked the fabric back.

A few seconds passed before her brain processed the scene. Huge chunks of fleshy meat covered the bottom of the tub. Sawed bone protruded, and muscle and veins dangled from the edges of the hacked carcass. A human finger became distinguishable. The wedding band still in place, gleamed in the light.

"Paul!" Margaret screamed.

Maya caught the horrified woman as she staggered back through the doorway and bumped into her. She clutched both of the woman's arms. "Thanks for the wonderful present," she said in a guttural tone.

Margaret's entire body convulsed. "What have you done to my Paul?" Her voice broke and trailed off with her son's name. Without restraint, tears flowed. "Let go of me, you... you monster."

She flung Margaret around and shoved with such force, the woman fell on the bed with a crack.

"Where ever did you find the impish doll? A wicked Santa?" Maya's eyes twinkled red, and her lips pulled into a malicious and hideous smile. "My favorite present from you, and I think Paul even enjoyed it for a little while."

Last night replayed in her mind. She was frightened by her husband and by the way he had glared at her. As he moved closer, his face had an unnatural, plastic-like sheen, and his eyes glowed red. The moment his mouth drew into the creepy Santa grin, she reacted. The corkscrew end of the bottle opener rammed into his temple. As she locked on Paul's shocked expression, a black wisp of smoke rose from him. It floated out of his lips and darted into hers. Now, she housed the doll's evil spirit.

Margaret struggled to get up. The fall caused an awkward twist in her spine and aggravated a lower lumbar injury from years ago. She couldn't move.

Maya grabbed the fireplace tool from its stand and glided toward the fractured woman. Her eyes glinted with a spark of red. "I have a gift for you, too." Maya thrust the metal point deep into the woman's abdomen. A contortion of pain overtook Margaret's face, and she winced as the hook withdrew. This gave Maya immense pleasure.

"Merry Christmas."

The poker dropped on the wooden floor with a clank, and Maya wrapped her fingers around Margaret's throat. She squeezed until the eyes promised to pop from their sockets. Each whimper that squeaked from Margaret brought delight as Maya choked the last bit of life from her.

"There," she said. Maya wiped her hands together free of the nasty deed. "I hope Paul hasn't grown too cold."

She sat at her table with a plate heaped of meat, garnished with the prepared vegetables, and ate.

The corner of the cloth napkin absorbed the grease from her lips. She finished her glass of Cabernet and gazed at the little stuffed figure in the chair beside her.

Maya picked the Santa up and peered into his bulb-like eyes. She blew the spirit back into the doll, kissed its plastic forehead, and whispered, "Until next Christmas…"

RELEVANT EVIDENCE

Content Warning: Criminal Violence, Kidnapping, Sexual Assault Against A Minor

We should have waited for the bus, but Emily wanted to walk. A proud third grader, and so confident she knew the way all by herself. There was no turning back. Her mind was made. Emily chose to disregard her mother's wish and headed toward the school on foot. A simple decision made in haste.

Our journey began on the corner, a block from home. Follow this street past the stoplight and turn right. Two more blocks to the dry cleaners. From there, we can cut across the parking lot. This part she repeated to solidify as truth. No thoughts were given to the rest of the directions, but she seemed to believe she would know the way once we got there.

After the last wrong turn, she no longer recognized where we were. The buildings appeared older, more abused than worn. Vacant windows provided the perfect space for eyes that leered and coveted. We moved fast, and her breath became quick and shallow. Panic rose as a reasonable response.

Behind us, someone stepped out from an alley, and the hairs on her legs stood. Emily sensed him, and I did too. *Don't look. Keep walking.* His scent now detectable as he neared us. He smelled stagnant and musky like something old and never used. He stalked us.

I wanted to shout but found no words for her to heed. Terror does that, takes the voice and leaves one silent. The situation left her primed to be plucked.

He's gone. Emily cried with relief, yet a fearfulness remained of never finding our way home. *Think. Read the signs.* Instead, she ran. Guard down. Full throttle in a direction farther from all things familiar. Feet pounding. Out of breath. Tears trailed.

Tires hummed toward us from the side street, and we stopped. I know Emily hoped it was help that approached, because I did. The lone car slowed, and a man peered from the driver's side through the rolled-down passenger window. It was the clerk from the dime store. To her, he sounded kind and polite when he asked if she was lost.

We shouldn't have gone with him. *No strangers.* A different choice never existed. He held the back door open, and we got in. She told him we lived on Maple Street. He replied, he already knew.

The door slammed. His fingers trailed the shape of the car as he strolled toward the other side. When he reached the hood, Emily tried the door latch, but like her mother's car, the safety lock had been engaged. The opposite rear door opened with a chilling click. He climbed in, over me, and straight on top of her.

A hand clamped her mouth while the other grabbed a leg. He dragged her down on the backseat. Without consent, he violated her in ways only a monster could. I don't know what was worse, having endured this offensive, or being forced to watch.

He left her, lying face down on the stained vinyl seat. Her nose pressed in the crease where the stench of soured milk, spilt on a summer day, drifted in the air. I stayed with her. Silent. Afraid of what he would do next.

Jostled by the motion, she glanced at me, eyes half-open. Crooked and twisted. I saw her mind work, not as a child, but as an animal desperate to be freed. The whirl of the tires switched to a rumple, followed by the crunch of gravel along an unknown path. Everything ended in an abrupt stop.

This was it. Her last chance. Not to live, she would never experience that, but to stay alive. Emily might, if all the stars aligned, manage to keep her life.

She pushed herself up and peeked out. The trunk popped, and she whipped around to the rear window. A sliver of daylight shone in until eclipsed by the bulk of him. He pulled on a pair of leather gloves. Her eyes darted and surveyed our surroundings, but she couldn't identify where we were.

She slipped over the seat back and onto the front seat. *Clever girl.* She opened the door. Not much, just the smallest amount possible to allow her petite frame through. She escaped and ran until her unlaced shoe flew off and tripped her. Hard fall. Loose dirt in mouth. Palms scraped.

He seized her, thrust his knee into her back, and pinned her down. No time for play. He snatched a fist full of hair and yanked her head back. The sun glinted on the blade as he dragged it across her neck. She convulsed, and her fragile body shuddered against me.

Material crinkled as he spread a tarp out and flung us together on the cold ground. Blood oozed from her tiny veins. A sharp rip of tape bound her arms to her side. Wrapped in black plastic and tied with a rope, he hauled us off.

Battered by jagged rocks, the plastic tore. Gouged. The jute abraded her skin. Without a mutter of sound from her tiny mouth, the details of our last moments became forever carved into her flesh. I wished she had seen, before I slipped away, that I had stayed with her as long as I could.

My displacement unnoticed, I watched her disappear, pulled along the ground like trash. I settled in the puddle where I fell. Abandoned. Lost. Left to rot on the wet soil. For days, maybe weeks, insects crawled around me. Over me. A predatory few encroached inside of me.

The light blue sky dissolved, and another night crept in. I wondered how our consciousness was linked because I believed she remained quite near.

Days. Nights. I stopped counting. Canine yelps trumpeted in the background. Voices clamored.

I chanted I'm here, wherever here was.

The dogs tracked me, and their barks grew louder as they trampled toward our scent.

Shrouded by blown leaves, I prayed they discovered me, and a cold nose grazed my toe.

They found me.

"Sarge! Over here!"

"Did you find something, Mick? What is it?"

"Not sure."

The officer lifted me from my grave. His eyes registered what he held, and he pushed his arm away from his body in disgust.

"Jesus, it's a little girl's sock, and it's covered with blood," he replied and dropped me into the evidence bag.

DEVILISH GAME

Published on CoffeeHouseWriters.com October 28 and November 11, 2019

"Most Views" Winner in both October and November 2019

Camille questioned her decision to bring someone to her home. But she had, and the girl's eagerness unsettled her. She stood at the corner and considered the possible outcomes.

Hair whipped around her face, and even with her eyes closed, tears formed with each icy gust. She didn't mind. Ever since she moved to Moondyne Falls earlier in the year, a daily ritual of crying had settled in.

"Come on," the girl called from two houses down.

Shades of ginger and golden brown drifted across the sidewalk and painted the lawns.

Fall bred optimism in Camille. A retraction of life through death and decay spawned hopefulness. After winter's gestation, life returned anew. This promise kept in blades of faded green that peeked through.

"Cam, I'm freezing."

The girl's name was Eleanor but insisted on Ellie. She also assigned a nickname for her, and with grace, Camille permitted this. She hoped it meant they were friends. So, she moved forward and joined her.

Three enormous steps led to a walkway, which ended with a flight of eight more. Limestone blocks created massive archways supported with ample columns. The same pale, gray rock covered the entire exterior.

From the street, the double doors at the entrance appeared at least eight-feet tall. Carved from thick slabs of mahogany and stained a deep, blood-red, they beckoned entry.

"Never been inside your house. Even when your grandfather passed. It sat vacant for weeks. Some kids from school wanted to sneak in, but I didn't." She smiled like her words merited some sort of prize.

"Armand Abraxas still lives here. My father is the one who died." Her eyes teared again. "I moved here to live with my grandfather."

They stared at the vast mansion, now her home. The idea of an intrusion made Camille's skin crawl. "He was only gone one week for the funeral." She took the first step.

"I don't think anyone did, though." Ellie paused on the path and gazed up.

Gargoyles, shaped from limestone, peered down from the tower's second story. At first, they would appear as lions. The longer one stared, the more sinister and monstrous they became. "I think they were too scared to break in," Ellie said as she caught up.

"Of what?"

"Ghosts." She waited as Camille unlocked the front door. "The Abraxas Castle is haunted. There are tons of books about it in the town's library."

Camille's face scrunched. The girl most likely wanted to say she had been inside—seen an apparition firsthand.

She opened the door and stepped inside. She walked through the vestibule and tossed her backpack on the seat of a bright red wooden chair.

A pair of brass, goat-like heads leered with a devilish smile. Both mounted where the stiles met the top rail. Their long, curled horns provided the perfect place for a scarf and coat.

"The architectural style is Romanesque."

Ellie's face lost all expression.

"Our house isn't a castle."

"Oh, right." Ellie tiptoed across the parquet floor and dropped her bag of textbooks on the chair next to Camille's. "Ooh. Is that a devil's head?"

"Where?" Camille followed her finger to where she pointed at one of the brass faces. "It's supposed to be Pan."

"Um…perhaps your house is full of mythological demons." Ellie drew her hands into claw-like shapes, pulled them next to her face, and gave her best moan. The sound echoed throughout the curved vestibule's doom.

"Sorry to disappoint you, but no ghosts or creatures. Only a bunch of family heirlooms like this weird chair." Camille took Ellie's coat and hung it from one of the horns.

"I don't believe in supernatural stuff." Ellie moved to the foot of the stairs and looked up. "But I am curious. Why are there so many stories about your house being haunted?"

"Are there?"

A memory slipped in of the summers she stayed with her father here. He read to her every night from her grandfather's secret book, but not about ghosts. The tales were fantastical and always about hunting evil. The image disappeared. "We should do our math assignment."

"We're not doing homework, Cam." Ellie traced the nose on the honey-colored man carved into the staircase post. "Got any games? Ouija would be fun."

Camille couldn't help but smile at her stupid grin. If having one friend pacified her grandfather, Eleanor Bridgeport would do. "I can find some cards." She led her into the parlor. "Let's sit here."

Ellie didn't sit. She wandered around the room. "Your house is like a time machine."

"Yeah, it was built in 1895. Most of the furniture is from the same period."

Camille pulled a tiny handle on one of the desk's miniature drawers. With no luck, she shoved it closed and slid the next one open. After two more attempts, she found a deck of Bicycle Playing Cards.

"So, no ghosts, but your grandfather is a tanner, right?

"He was. He's retired now."

"Well, the story goes that he killed several members of the Moondyne family. He tanned their skin. Then, he made papyrus for his handmade journals. That's where he recorded how he murdered them."

"What are you talking about?" Camille laughed as she sat on the handwoven rug next to the cocktail table and shuffled the cards. "None of that is real, besides papyrus paper is from a plant. Parchment is buckskin, but untanned."

A display of ancient weapons mounted on the wall drew Ellie's attention. "Isn't your family in some centuries-long battle with the Moondynes, though? A feud over who founded the town?"

The shiny blade of a Rapier sword tempted her, so she reached a finger out.

"I wouldn't," Camille said.

She retracted her hand. "Why?"

"What has gotten into you? I thought we were playing Rummy or something."

"Well, this makes me wonder whether the legend is true."

"What legend?"

"If a member of the Abraxas family is in the proximity of one of the Moondynes, they must fight."

She stared back at her. "Are you crazy? I'm not fighting anyone. Those are rumors— all make-believe."

Ellie raised her brows and glanced at the collection of weapons.

"I didn't want you to knock them down." Camille got up. "I don't plan on being near them. They can keep their claim as founders."

"What about Debbie?" Ellie didn't wait for a reply. "I invited her over."

"Here? To my house?" Camille's hands clenched into tight fists, and her cheeks warmed. "Why did you invite her?"

"You like her. She's normal, and she's not related to them or to you." She offered her best pout. "You're making friends. Remember?"

She hated it, but Ellie was right. If Camille didn't lighten up and embrace Moondyne Falls, her entire senior year would suck. The first half had been tragic enough, and, if alive, her father would have encouraged her to fit in.

"Cam?" She snapped her fingers. "Hello?"

"Fine, we'll play cards with Debbie."

"Great. Do you have any snacks?"

"Yeah." Camille crossed the room, and a need to exert some measure of control overcame her. She turned. "You got me in this mess, so you can help."

"Sure."

On the far side of the dining room, a narrow door led to the mansion's kitchen. "Grab some sodas from the fridge."

Ellie obeyed.

Camille dumped a bag of potato chips into a silver, claw foot bowl. She didn't dare look over at her new friend. A quizzical expression would be smeared across her face about the chosen dish.

She headed back to the front of the house down the long, paneled hallway. Her friend tagged behind. "Don't worry, Cam. Debbie is fun."

Halfway to the parlor, the doorbell rang.

"She's here."

Camille froze as the hairs on her arms raised a warning.

"Want me to answer it?"

No words escaped Camille's mouth. So, Ellie unlatched the bolt and pulled the heavy wooden door open. "Hey, Debbie." She gestured for her to enter.

Debbie glanced over her left shoulder, and Ellie leaned out. She peered around the door frame to see who or what was there. "Ooh, this isn't good."

Tiffany Moondyne stepped around them and waltzed inside Camille's home.

"Wow," Tiffany said. "How perfectly medieval."

"Romanesque," Ellie corrected with a nervous smile. She took the chips from Camille and whispered, "She's a bitch, but she throws the best Halloween parties."

Ellie headed to the front room. "Everything's ready. Come on. The party is in here."

Under intense scrutiny, Tiffany acted coy, but Camille sensed something darker in her actions.

"What's this room?" Tiffany asked. She stood outside Camille's grandfather's study. The toe of both her shoes were centimeters from the room's threshold.

"We're playing Rummy in this room, Tiff," Ellie said.

"She won't go in." Camille didn't know how she knew, but it was the truth. Confident, she returned and joined the others.

Tiffany spun around. "Cards are for babies." She sauntered toward them but paused at the foot of the staircase. Fixated on something ahead, she said, "I found something better."

The three girls kept their eyes on Tiffany as she walked past the parlor and disappeared. Seconds later, backpacks thudded on the wood, and an ear-piercing screech made them cringe.

Having removed everything, Tiffany dragged the red chair into the center of the hall.

"You're scratching the floor." Camille raced toward Tiffany.

An urge to throw this rude interloper out of her house rose within Camille. The thought generated a smirk. If all the Moondynes acted like this, it was no wonder battles erupted.

"I have my own game for us to play." Tiffany signaled for Camille to take a seat.

Camille scoffed and turned around and almost ran into Ellie and Debbie, who stood close behind.

Desperate to lighten the mood, Ellie rushed over and sat in the devil-headed chair. "What do I have to do?"

"Simple, I ask a question, and you answer." Tiffany tapped her lip with her pink-polished fingernail.

"Like truth or dare?" Ellie's voice quivered.

Tiffany grinned. "Kind of, but the dare part is the sitting." She locked eyes with Camille. "If you lie, the devil takes your soul to hell."

"This is stupid. We're not doing this. Get up, Ellie."

"What's my question?"

"Do you really like Camille, or did you just want inside her house?"

Camille's eyes cut to her supposed friend, who squirmed on the red seat. She feared as much but wanted her to say it.

"A little of both, I guess." She got up. "Sorry, Cam."

Tiffany presented a devilish grin. "Now you, Camille."

"I told you. I'm not playing."

Debbie volunteered to go next and moved forward.

"No!" Tiffany snatched Camille by her sleeve, pulled her in. "Camille's turn!"

The Abraxas medallion around Camille's neck glowed with warmth and tingled her skin. She tucked the heirloom necklace inside her shirt before she seized Tiffany's hand.

Camille flung the obnoxious girl away.

Tiffany screamed as she fell on the chair. She twisted and writhed like something possessed her. She collapsed on the seat and squealed in pain.

"Eww, what reeks?" Ellie asked.

Debbie raced to the poor girl's side, but smoke rolled from under her friend's thighs and halted her action.

The brass, curled horns wiggled as the piece of furniture seared through her tights and scorched her flesh. Pan had awakened.

Tiffany's face contorted, and she hissed.

Camille grabbed her by the ankles and glanced up before she pulled. For a second, a flash of raw leathery fibers stretched across the girl's cheek. Embers for eyes glared back from the demon.

She yanked with such excessive force, the demon-possessed girl flew off the chair. The back of Tiffany's head whacked against the seat's edge as she plummeted down before her whole body resting lifeless on the parquet floor.

The three girls stared at the uninvited, snobbish girl splayed at their feet. Camille was sure only she held this sentiment. Tiffany had received an invitation from Debbie, who had been invited by Ellie, whose friendship she questioned.

In observation, Tiffany Moondyne appeared normal, or as normal as an unconscious person could. None the less, the girls' true nature exposed itself in the raw, leathery fibers coated in bloody slime which stretched across her cheeks. The eyes had glared back like hot embers from a hellish fire.

Camille knelt beside her and placed her hand on the pale cheekbone where only moments ago a devil flashed.

"Is she dead? Did you kill her?" Ellie paced behind the chair.

"No." She didn't believe so, but she leaned over, her ear near Tiffany's nose and mouth, and listened. "She's breathing."

The family medallion slid free from Camille's shirt and dangled inches above the girl's body. She realized the prickle on her skin stopped the moment the girl became insentient.

"What's this?" Armand Abraxas stood in the vestibule, and his towering shadow pierced the hall. He removed his overcoat and draped it over the stair rail.

"Grandpa," Camille said, startled by his entrance. She glanced at the other two girls and back at him. "Tiffany fell, and..."

"Tiffany?" His eyes cut to his granddaughter as he raced over. He bent down and cradled her head with one of his hands. "This girl is a Moondyne."

Debbie seized the opportunity and slipped out while Camille and her grandfather focused on the injured girl.

"Yeah, I know, but I didn't bring her here."

"Doesn't matter. No one is allowed inside. Help me lift her up."

The afternoon's events replayed in her mind.

"Camille?"

This time she responded and grabbed Tiffany's arm, surprised to find Ellie next to her helping. They lifted Tiffany, and this motion caused the girl to stir.

"Put her in the chair," Armand instructed

"No." Camille pulled them toward the parlor. "On the sofa."

He glanced at the red seat and then back at his granddaughter. "Camille, has something gone on here I need to be aware of?"

"Other than Cam trying to kill our classmate?" Ellie displayed her stupid grin at the aged man.

"Who is this?" Armand demanded.

Camille moved to the hallway and stood in front of the piece of furniture in question. She sensed her grandfather's approach. "Grandpa, I think I'm seeing things."

His arm stretched around her shoulders, and he squeezed her

close. "Grief is a terrible beast and consumes you if you're not careful. Believe me, I suffer this too."

The loss of her father had broken her heart, but this conveyed something different: more tangible, more real. "The horns on Pan wiggled, and when Tiffany fell on the seat, her skin burnt."

He studied the pair of brass goat heads. "I hoped I wouldn't need to tell you so soon, but I fear time has run out. There is much about your heritage you must learn." He gazed at the Abraxas stone hanging from her neck. "Tell me, did it glow?"

Camille looked down at the polished green gemstone. "Uh, yeah." She had never examined the symbol engraved into the stone. Now the image of a rooster-headed man with split legs like serpents struck her as rather conspicuous.

"It tingled your skin?"

"Yes." She clasped the medallion in her hand and pressed it against her chest. "What is it?"

"I plan to explain, but first..."

The doorbell rang, and Ellie raced to answer it.

"What now?"

"Mr. Abraxas, it's Tiffany's mom."

"Armand," the woman said, cloaked in a red, wool cape with white rabbit fur collar and cuffs. Debbie, who returned with her, peeked with sheepish eyes from behind the woman where she hid.

"Seren Moondyne," he said as he marched toward his front door, "your daughter is fine. I agree to pay for any medical treatment, of course, if required."

Ellie led her to the parlor, and the woman released a sardonic laugh as she passed Armand. "Your granddaughter broke our centuries-long truce in a matter of months after moving here."

"Be mindful of your words, Seren." He studied her as she hovered over her daughter reposed upon his couch.

"Mother?" Tiffany asked.

"I'm informed of what transpired here today. This girl," she said, pointing her bony finger at Debbie, "informed me Camille lured them into your home. All under the pretense of making friends and playing games." Seren turned to cast disapproval upon Camille.

She stepped forward. "I didn't invite her here, and I didn't want any of this. I wanted to do my math homework."

Ellie glanced down.

Camille hoped her friend suffered from overwhelming guilt.

"You played games, didn't you?" Mrs. Moondyne asked.

"The only sport here is the devilish game your daughter played. Camille knew nothing."

"Well, she must. I see the burns on Tiffany and don't think for a moment I'm not aware of the horrific stories about Pan and your chair."

"Pan cannot be awakened without a demon present. You know that."

Ellie, left to nurse Tiffany, pulled the glass of water from the girl's lips and stepped away. "Um, Cam? I'm gonna go." Ellie snatched her coat and scarf off the floor and fled, but no one cared.

"I witnessed your daughter's true self." Camille, convinced her mind had not tricked her, became emboldened by this truth.

"It is your daughter, Mrs. Moondyne, who broke our pact, and you must leave here before I insist my granddaughter to finish her sworn duty."

Seren glanced back at her daughter, now off the couch and moving toward her. "This means war, Armand. We are at war."

The front door slammed behind the woman and the two girls as they left The Abraxas Castle.

"What did Tiffany's mother mean?" Camille trailed behind her grandfather as he aggressively paced toward his study.

"The Moondyne and Abraxas families have fought each other since the beginning of time. Darkness versus light, and all, but three hundred years ago, we signed a pact. They agreed to never invoke demons, and we would keep all higher beings with sworn allegiance to our family at bay. The Moondyne's one contingency was they were recorded as the town founders, instead of us."

"Light and dark, good and evil, a little prosaic, isn't it? What's really going on?"

"I'm trying to tell you, Camille, we're demon hunters, and the necklace—it's proof of our legacy. Abraxas is the name of the highest god. The one complete, undivided, and unified. An aspect of this high being split into good and evil. We are unconcerned with the souls who balance on the line. If they chose darkness, we must return their shadow back to the source. This is an opportunity for rebirth into the light once again." He raced to his desk and pulled out his locked, handmade journal.

He seized a vial full of white grains from a wooden box next to his lamp.

"What's that for?"

"Pan must be contained in the chair. If he escapes, there is no controlling his actions." Armand glanced at his granddaughter. "I'm sorry you weren't told, but I never imagined your father would die before me."

She studied her grandfather. "Grandpa, you should lie down. You're right, the grief is too much. Your thinking isn't clear."

"Camille, we don't have the luxury of time. You must trust me." Armand circled the red chair and sprinkled the coarse salt on the floor. He opened his book, searched for the binding spell, and recited the words.

They waited.

The chair did nothing.

"Too late. Pan freed himself while we became distracted."

"What do we do now?"

"We wait for his next move. I have not encountered this myself. No one has, not for centuries. I'm afraid he holds the cards." Armand picked the chair up and placed it against the wall near the vestibule.

"Isn't Pan incorruptible?"

"Everything contains a shadow. Three hundred years trapped inside a piece of furniture, hard to conceive what he's planned."

He headed down the hallway. "We can talk more over dinner."

"I'm not hungry."

"You must keep your strength."

"For what? To kill Tiffany Moondyne? Are we murderers?"

"No, actually, we're servants of the Most-High. I don't expect you to go on faith. You experienced the medallion's reaction when a demon became a threat to you. You can't deny that."

"I didn't ask for any of this." Camille turned away from her grandfather and headed toward the stairs. "I'm going up to my room." She grabbed the banister and paused at the man's face carved into the honey-colored wood. She didn't touch it. How many other creatures were trapped in the confines of her home? She remembered the stone gargoyles, and a shiver rushed through her.

She plopped face down on her antique, four-poster bed prepared for a long, ritual cry. All she could think about was Tiffany and the demon she witnessed hidden within. What was she supposed to do? Go to school, and when she ran into the girl, battle her to the death right there?

Memories filled her mind, and her tears flowed. She didn't understand why her father never told her. This new responsibility weighed on Camille. Her father's passing must have activated her powers or the Abraxas stone he gave her did. She lifted the chain over her head and laid the necklace on her pillow.

A silhouette flitted across her left peripheral vision, and her head jerked in its direction. Nothing. She slid to the edge of her bed, afraid to let her foot down to the floor. "Oh, this is ridiculous," she said.

She stood, took the medallion, and stowed it in the nightstand's drawer.

"You shouldn't take that off. Ever."

Camille spun around. A creature waited in her bedroom, and she was convinced it was a hallucination. Her eyes scanned his thick, muscular hindquarters and legs with hoofed feet. His torso was of a man, and his face and head a hybrid blend of both man and goat. She chuckled. This is what the Greek myth looked like to her.

"You're not frightened?"

"You're an illusion."

"Is that so?" Pan ran his finger down the length of her arm. "That felt quite real, didn't it?"

"I thought you were a god?"

"I am, of shepherds and hunters." He moved in closer, his bare chest centimeters from hers, and his breath hot across her face. "And, you're a hunter."

"Why are you here?"

"You mean in general or in your private quarters?"

"Both." She sat on her bed to create some distance between them. He joined her, and she understood her mistake.

"I am bound when evoked, but neither you nor your grandfather called for me. As for you, your medallion is what protects you from possession— both good and evil."

He pushed her on to the bed and forced his mouth on hers. She resisted but found his kiss intoxicating. She surrendered, and at that moment, unprotected by the Abraxas stone, he dematerialized, and his spirit disappeared through her lips like a swirl of smoke.

Camille, empowered by this god, understood. The demons were the decayed leaves. Their death-like winter's slumber, and hope for their soul's restoration. She was the restorer of fallen souls.

Tomorrow, she would apologize to Tiffany. Pan would help secure an invitation to the Halloween party. Tiff won't be able to say no. Once there, she could finish off the Moondyne clan.

ABOUT THE AUTHOR

*"Words have no power to impress the mind without
the exquisite horror of their reality."*
-Edgar Allan Poe

Julie Kusma, author of *Shift: 11 Perspective Changing Meditations* and *Unbind 7 Chakra Opening Meditations*, lives in Kentucky with her family and Goldendoodle, Finn. She writes speculative fiction short stories, primarily horror, science fiction, and supernatural. She also writes metaphysical content such as her CDs which are available everywhere music is sold.

Sign up for updates and links to her latest works at
http://juliekusma.com

and **follow** Julie on
http://twitter.com/juliekusma
https://www.pinterest.com/juliekusma/
https://www.linkedin.com/in/julie-kusma/
http://instagram.com/juliekusma
https://www.goodreads.com/user/julie-kusma

Printed in Great Britain
by Amazon

18692919R00047